IF I MET AN ICE AGE ANIMAL

# IF I DINED WITH DIRE WOLVES

by Jenna Lee Gleisner
illustrated by Michelle Simpson

GRASSHOPPER

## Tools for Parents & Teachers

Grasshopper Books enhance imagination and introduce the earliest readers to fiction with fun storylines and illustrations. The easy-to-read text supports early reading experiences with repetitive sentence patterns and sight words.

### Before Reading

- Discuss the cover illustration. What do readers see?
- Look at the picture glossary together. Discuss the words.

### Read the Book

- Read the book to the child, or have him or her read independently.
- "Walk" through the book and look at the illustrations. Who is the main character? What is happening in the story?

### After Reading

- Prompt the child to think more. Ask: The main character imagines hunting with a pack of dire wolves. If you could spend a day with a group of animals, what group would it be? What would you do with them?

Grasshopper Books are published by Jump!
5357 Penn Avenue South
Minneapolis, MN 55419
www.jumplibrary.com



Library of Congress Cataloging-in-Publication Data

Names: Gleisner, Jenna Lee, author.
Simpson, Michelle, illustrator.
Title: If I dined with dire wolves / by Jenna Lee Gleisner;
illustrated by Michelle Simpson.
Description: Minneapolis, MN: Jump!, Inc., 2023.
Series: If I met an Ice Age animal | Includes index.
Audience: Ages 5-8.
Identifiers: LCCN 2021060744 (print)
LCCN 2021060745 (ebook)
ISBN 9781636909394 (hardcover)
ISBN 9781636909400 (paperback)
ISBN 9781636909417 (ebook)
Subjects: CYAC: Dire wolf–Fiction. | Wolves–Fiction.
Prehistoric animals–Fiction. | LCGFT: Picture books.
Classification: LCC PZ7.1.G5885 If 2023 (print)
LCC PZ7.1.G5885 (ebook)
DDC [E]–dc23
LC record available at https://lccn.loc.gov/2021060744
LC ebook record available at https://lccn.loc.gov/2021060745

Editor: Eliza Leahy
Direction and Layout: Anna Peterson
Illustrator: Michelle Simpson

Printed in the United States of America at
Corporate Graphics in North Mankato, Minnesota.

# Table of Contents

# Part of the Pack

"Mom, we learned about dire wolves today!" my twin brother says.

"Would they have eaten soup for dinner, too?" she asks.

“No, Mom. They lived 10,000 years ago during the Ice Age. They dined on wild horses and giant ground sloths!” he says.

*What if* I *dined with dire wolves?*
I wonder.

If I dined with dire wolves,
I would bundle up.

During the Ice Age,
everything was covered
in ice and snow. *Brr!*

Dire wolves had thick
fur to keep them warm.

We would hunt! Dire wolves were carnivores. They lived and hunted in packs. A pack could have up to 30 wolves.

If I hunted with dire wolves, I would hear them howl.

*Awoooooo!*

One of the wolves found dinner!

We would run to him. Dire wolves were fast and strong. I'd run fast to keep up.

The pack found a giant ground sloth to eat. If I hunted with dire wolves, I might see a short-faced bear. These bears hunted giant ground sloths, too. But hunting in a pack helps the wolves.

Dinnertime!

short-faced bear
giant ground sloth

After the hunt, I would follow the pack to its den.

den

The wolves would cut the food with their big, strong teeth. Then they would share it with me.

"No, thank you!" I'd say. "My mom is making food at home!"

Even the pups would get some.

If I dined with dire wolves, we would nap after. Some wolves would chew on the bones.

*Slurp!*

Then I hear another slurp.

"Yum!" says my brother. "Why aren't you eating?"

"I was imagining dining with dire wolves," I say.

"You can't. They're extinct!" he says.

# Parts of a Dire Wolf

Dire wolves weighed up to 175 pounds (79 kilograms). They were about six feet (1.8 meters) long from snout to tail. Take a look at the parts of a dire wolf.

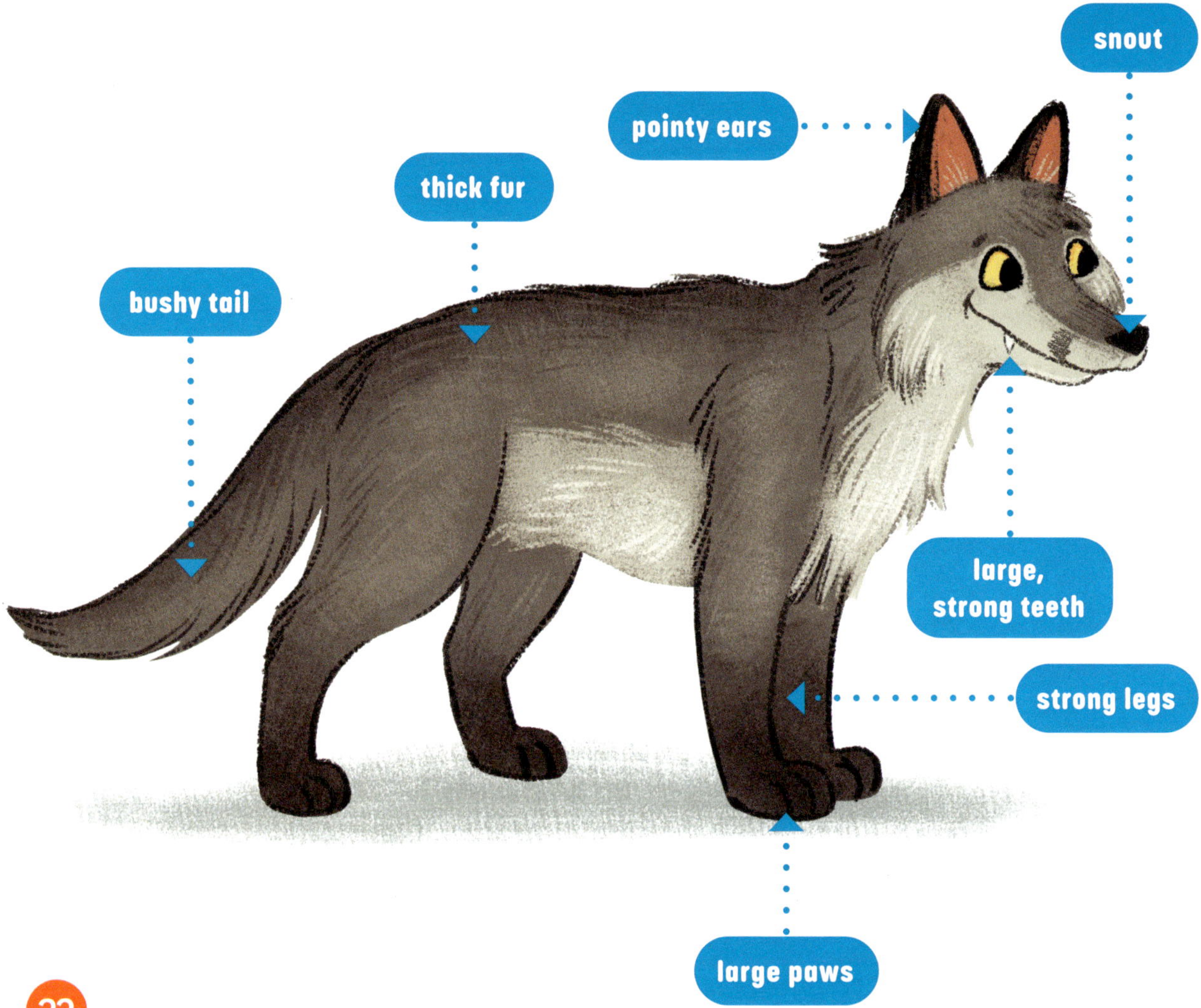

# Picture Glossary

**carnivores**
Animals that eat meat.

**extinct**
No longer found alive and known about only through fossils or history.

**howl**
To make a long, loud cry.

**Ice Age**
A period of time, about 10,000 years ago, when a large part of Earth was covered with ice.

**packs**
Groups of dire wolves.

**pups**
Baby dire wolves.

# Index



# To Learn More

**Finding more information is as easy as 1, 2, 3.**

1. Go to www.factsurfer.com
2. Enter "**ifIdinedwithdirewolves**" into the search box.
3. Choose your book to see a list of websites.

# KENYA

By Anna Collins
and Alicia Z. Klepeis

EXPLORING WORLD CULTURES

Cavendish Square

Published in 2024 by Cavendish Square Publishing, LLC
2544 Clinton Street, Buffalo, NY 14224



Second Edition



Library of Congress Cataloging-in-Publication Data
Names: Collins, Anna, author. | Klepeis, Alicia, 1971- author.
Title: Kenya / by Anna Collins and Alicia Z. Klepeis.
Other titles: Exploring world cultures.
Description: 2nd ed. | Buffalo, NY : Cavendish Square Publishing, 2024. | Series: Exploring world cultures | Includes bibliographical references and index.
Identifiers: LCCN 2023032790 | ISBN 9781502669964 (library binding) | ISBN 9781502669957 (paperback) | ISBN 9781502669971 (ebook)
Subjects: LCSH: Kenya--Juvenile literature. | Kenya--Civilization--Juvenile literature.
Classification: LCC DT433.522 .K54 2024 | DDC 967.62--dc23
LC record available at https://lccn.loc.gov/2023032790

Writers: Alicia Z. Klepeis; Anna Collins (second edition)
Editor: Jennifer Lombardo
Copyeditor: Danielle Haynes
Designer: Andrea Davison-Bartolotta

The photographs in this book are used by permission and through the courtesy of: Cover Lucian Coman/Shutterstock.com; p. 4 Volodymyr Burdiak/Shutterstock.com; p. 5 Jen Watson/Shutterstock.com; p. 6 Sebastian Castelier/Shutterstock.com; p. 7 Dimitrios Karamitros/Shutterstock.com; p. 8 Danny Ye/Shutterstock.com; p. 9 Alexandros Michailidis/Shutterstock.com; p. 10 Sopotnicki/Shutterstock.com; p. 11 Syrus Neilson/Shutterstock.com; p. 12 Lidia Daskalova/Shutterstock.com; p. 13 Mary MM/Shutterstock.com; p. 15 (bottom) Anna Om/Shutterstock.com; p. 15 (top) Ana Gram/Shutterstock.com; p. 16 ANDRZEJ GRZEGORCZYK/Shutterstock.com; p. 17 jo Crebbin/Shutterstock.com; p. 18 Elen Marlen/Shutterstock.com; p. 19 Vlad Karavaev/Shutterstock.com; p. 20 SeeSaw GmbH/Shutterstock.com; p. 21 FOTOGRIN/Shutterstock.com; p. 22 mark stephens photography/Shutterstock.com; p. 23 Oleg_Mit/Shutterstock.com; p. 24 Aleksandar Todorovic/Shutterstock.com; p. 25 Laiotz/Shutterstock.com; p. 26 Alex Mwai/Shutterstock.com; p. 27 Papa Bravo/Shutterstock.com; p. 28 Andrzej Kubik/Shutterstock.com; p. 29 bonchan/Shutterstock.com.



CPSIA compliance information: Batch #CW24CSQ: For further information contact Cavendish Square Publishing LLC at 1-877-980-4450.

Printed in the United States of America

# CONTENTS

# INTRODUCTION

Africa is a **continent** that looks different all over. However, when people think of Africa, they often imagine Kenya. Its grassy **savannas** have been used in many movies and TV shows. Humans have lived in Kenya for millions of years, but it wasn't always the country we know today.

Kenyans have many kinds of jobs. Many people grow food or raise animals on farms. Others work in

*This picture shows giraffes on the savanna with Mount Kilimanjaro in the background. The mountain is in Tanzania, but it can be seen from Kenya as well.*

factories, hotels, or schools. Kenya has a problem with wealth inequality. This means that the gap between the richest and poorest people is very large.

Kenya has mountains, grasslands, beaches, and deserts. People come from all over the world to see Kenya's wildlife. The country is home to more than 50 national parks and **reserves**. People also visit Nairobi and Mombasa, its two largest cities.

Like all countries, Kenya has some problems. However, the people of Kenya are proud of their country and are working to make it the best it can be.

*There are tea farms in western Kenya. These women are picking tea leaves.*

# GEOGRAPHY

Kenya is about twice the size of the U.S. state of Nevada. It covers 224,081 square miles (580,367 square kilometers) in East Africa. Its capital city is Nairobi.

**FACT!**
*October and February are Kenya's hottest months. It can get up to 90 degrees Fahrenheit (32 degrees Celsius).*

*Women take water from Lake Victoria for their families. Many Kenyan houses don't have running water.*

Kenya is bordered by Ethiopia, Somalia, South Sudan, Tanzania, and Uganda. The Indian Ocean is to the east. Lake Victoria is to the west. Near the Indian Ocean, the land is flat and grassy. The ground rises toward the center of the country. This place is called the highlands. Most Kenyans live in this area.

Kenya is close to the **equator**. This makes it hot all year long. The hottest part of the country is near the coast.

## THE GREAT RIFT VALLEY

The Great Rift Valley is west of Nairobi. This valley is 4,000 miles (6,400 km) long. A lot of plants grow there, so it's very green. It's also a little cooler there than in other parts of the country.

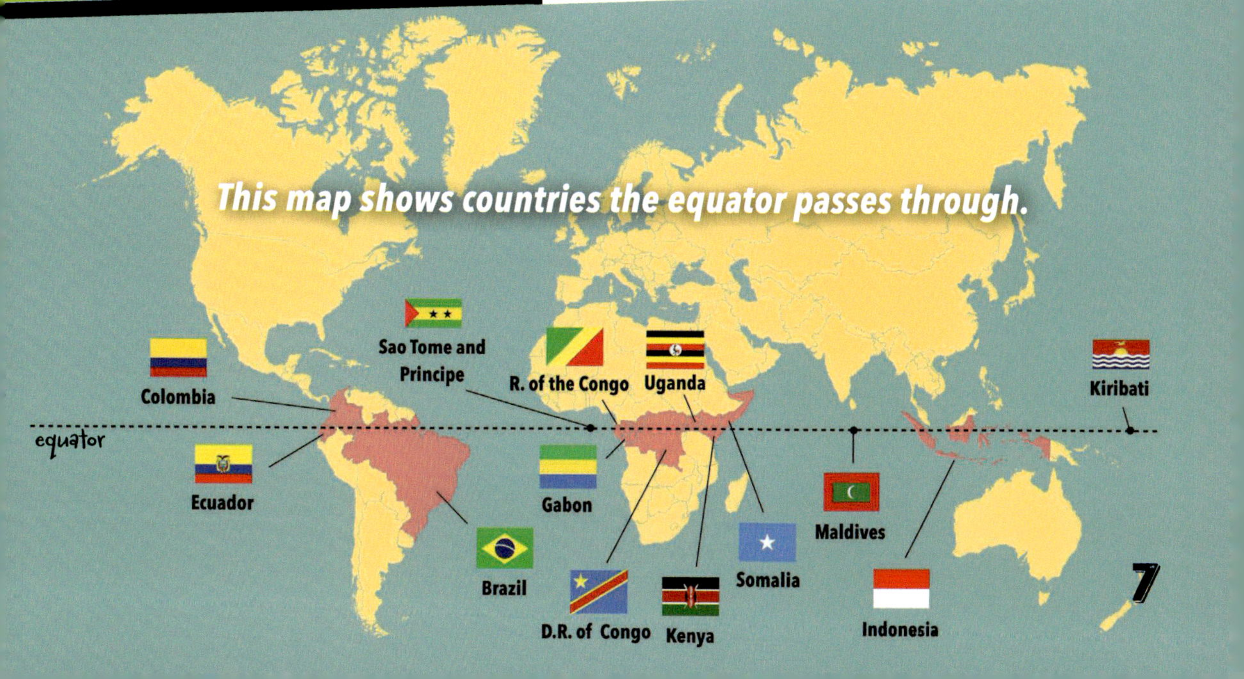


This map shows countries the equator passes through.

# HISTORY

Scientists know that all human life started in Africa. Kenya may have been one of the places where the earliest humans lived.

At least 1,400 years ago, Arabs started settling near Kenya's coasts. They built trading places there. This led to contact with people from India, Persia, and other Arab areas. Many of these groups enslaved Kenyans and sent them to other parts of the world.

***This picture shows a model of a 1.8-million-year-old skull from an early human relative that a Kenyan scientist found in 1973.***

## PRE-HUMAN FOSSILS

Scientists have found the earliest hominin **fossils** in Kenya. Hominins were early relatives of humans. Over time, they evolved, or changed, into humans as we are today.

In 1498, the Portuguese tried to take over Kenya's coastal areas. They failed, but the British were able to take over all of Kenya in 1895. They ruled Kenya until 1963.

**FACT!**

In 1952, a group called the Mau Mau tried to take Kenya back from the British. The British killed many Kenyans while trying to keep their power.

*Kenya has had five presidents since 1964. Kenyans elected William Ruto (shown here) in 2022.*

# GOVERNMENT

Kenya is split into 47 parts called counties. Each one has its own local government. There's also a central government that controls the whole country. Kenyans vote for their leaders.

The Kenyan government has three branches. The legislative branch is called Parliament. It writes the laws. It's made up of two parts. As of 2023, the Senate has 67 members, and the National Assembly has 349 members. Parliament meets in Nairobi.

*This picture shows the Parliament buildings in Nairobi.*

The judicial branch makes sure the laws are fair. It's made up of the courts. The executive branch is made up of the president, vice president, and **cabinet**. They make sure people follow the laws.

## UNFAIR ELECTIONS

From 1969 to 1992, elections in Kenya weren't fair. There was only one choice for president, so it didn't matter who people wanted to vote for. After 1992, people had more choices again.

**FACT!**

The **constitution** Kenya follows today was written in 2010.

*This picture shows a monument of Jomo Kenyatta, Kenya's first president.*

# THE ECONOMY

Kenya has the biggest **economy** in East Africa. It is made up of several different parts, or sectors. Farming makes up the biggest sector of the economy. Kenyan farmers grow tea, flowers, and coffee that are sold around the world. They also grow food for themselves. In cities, many Kenyans work in hospitals, schools, and banks.

**FACT!**

*Kenya is one of only a few countries in the world to grow purple tea. It gets its name from the color of its leaves.*

*This picture shows a greenhouse full of roses on a Kenyan flower farm.*

Manufacturing, or making things in factories, is the second-biggest sector. Factory workers make things such as clothes, furniture, and plastic items.

The third-biggest sector is tourism. Tourists are people who visit another country for fun. Many Kenyans serve tourists in stores, hotels, and places to eat.

*Kenya's money is called the shilling.*

### BRINGING ITEMS IN

Something one country buys from another is called an import. Some of Kenya's main imports are machines, cars, and oil. Some of its top trading partners are India, China, and South Africa.

# THE ENVIRONMENT

Kenya has many beautiful plants and animals. These include elephants, lions, leopards, buffalo, and rhinoceroses. Some of these animals are in danger because of humans. Poachers are people who illegally hunt animals. Humans have also moved onto some animals' land. This makes it harder for the animals to find food.

**FACT!**
The Meru oak is a large tree that grows only in Kenya.

Cities have different problems. Gas from cars pollutes the air, or makes it dirty. Some people also burn plastics to get rid of trash.

Many Kenyans do not have clean water. Some water is polluted by waste from farms and factories. In other places, trash and human waste pollute the water.

## CLIMATE CHANGE

All over the world, the **climate** is changing because of things humans are doing. One of Kenya's biggest problems from climate change is drought, or long periods without rain.

*This picture shows a male and female lion at Maasai Mara National Reserve.*

*Large groups of flamingos live in Lake Nakuru.*

# THE PEOPLE TODAY

Kenya is home to many different **ethnic groups**. No single group in Kenya makes up a majority of the nation's population. Each one has its own culture, or way of life. The Kikuyu people make up about 17 percent of Kenyans. In the past, they had no written language. They kept their culture alive through stories, dances, and songs.

**FACT!**
About 57 million people live in Kenya.

*Some Kikuyu people paint their faces and wear large collars around their necks. However, many Kenyans dress in Western-style clothes, especially in the cities.*

The Luhya people make up about 14 percent of Kenya's population. Many smaller groups make up the Luhya. The Luo people, who make up about 10 percent of the population, live outside the cities. They often fish in Lake Victoria. Other ethnic groups include the Kalenjin, Kisii, and Meru peoples.

*The pattern of beads on this Maasai woman's clothing shows that she is a respected member of her community.*

## THE MAASAI PEOPLE

The Maasai people live in a huge area of southern Kenya and Tanzania. Cattle ownership is a big part of their culture. They are well known for their beautiful bead art.

# LIFESTYLE

Life in Kenya is different depending on where someone lives. About 75 percent of Kenyans live in rural, or country, areas. These people often make a living by farming. Some grow crops or raise animals to sell. Others grow food to feed their families. Kenyans who live in cities live more like people in the United States.

*These Maasai men are making a fire without matches.*

**FACT!**

Teenagers in Kenya are only allowed to be around teens of a different gender when an adult is around. High schools are for all girls or all boys.

Nairobi has many large, modern buildings.

No matter where they live, Kenyans share many of the same values. For example, family is very important in Kenya. Aunts, uncles, and cousins often stop by without calling first. They visit with the parents and help raise the children. Family members share food and clothes with each other all the time.

## NO PRIVACY? NO PROBLEM

In Kenya, privacy, or being left alone, is not common. Kenyans are always around friends and family unless they're sleeping. Unlike in the United States, a person's bedroom isn't considered a private space, so kids don't spend much time alone in their room.

# RELIGION

More than 85 percent of Kenyans are Christian. Most of them are Protestant. There is also a large number of Catholic people in Kenya. About 11 percent of Kenyans are Muslim. All other religions, or belief systems, make up less than 2 percent of the population.

**FACT!**
*A very small number of Kenyans say they have no religion.*

Church is an important part of life for many Kenyan Christians.

Before outsiders came to Kenya, each tribe, or group, had its own faith. Many believed in one god. They also believed that the spirits of their **ancestors** needed to be given certain gifts to keep them happy. If the spirits were unhappy, they could bring sickness or bad luck to the tribe. Many Kenyans—even Christians—still believe this today.

## INDIAN RELIGIONS

The British controlled Kenya and India at the same time. When the British wanted a railway built in Kenya, they brought in Indian workers. Many stayed in Kenya when the railway was finished. Today, many Indians living in Kenya follow Indian faiths such as Hinduism.

*Kenyan Muslims often visit a mosque such as this one to pray.*

# LANGUAGE

Kenya has two official languages: English and Kiswahili. An official language is one that's used by the government. Big Kenyan companies that do business outside Kenya also use English.

**FACT!**

Kiswahili is also known as Swahili. It is spoken by the Swahili people.

*This sign is written in both English and Kiswahili.*

## NO WORRIES

The Disney movie *The Lion King* uses many Kiswahili words. Most of the characters' names are Kiswahili. For example, Simba means lion, and Rafiki means friend. The song "Hakuna Matata" comes from a real Kiswahili phrase that means "no worries."

Kiswahili is a Bantu language. People speak this language in much of East Africa and in South Africa. It is often used in small businesses throughout Kenya.

Students learn both English and Kiswahili in primary schools. TV and radio shows often use both languages too. Although these are the two main languages, there are as many as 70 spoken throughout the country. Many Kenyans speak English, Kiswahili, and the language that belongs to their ethnic group.

Kenya's government prints money with English and Kiswahili words on it.

# ARTS AND FESTIVALS

Art and music are very important in Kenyan culture. Artists make pots, beaded clothing, masks, and more. Different ethnic groups in Kenya have their own unique, or special, music. People often play music during special events or when dancing.

Kenya also has many festivals each year. One of the largest is the three-day Turkana festival in June. People from all the **nomadic** communities in northern Kenya gather to share their cultures.

*Some Kenyan artists make many different kinds of masks.*

Many Kenyan songs have drums in them.

## ROCK ART

In some places throughout Kenya, visitors can see rock art that is millions of years old. These include pictures of animals and circular shapes. Ancient people drew on the rocks with a type of clay paint. They **engraved** others, possibly with sharp sticks.

Independence Day (also called Jamhuri Day) is on December 12. This holiday marks the day in 1963 when Kenya became an independent country. Kenyans have parades and parties with lots of food and dancing.

**FACT!**
A Kenyan company called Ocean Sole turns used flip-flops into art to help the environment.

# FUN AND PLAY

Like people all over the world, Kenyans like to have fun. They enjoy playing sports, especially soccer. They play this game in the countryside as well as in cities. People also like to watch sports on TV.

Many Kenyans hike and camp in the country's national parks and reserves. There are also beautiful beaches to visit.

**FACT!**
Mount Kenya is 17,057 feet (5,199 meters) tall.

Many Kenyans enjoy hiking near Mount Kenya (shown here).

There are many things to do in the cities for people who can afford it. Playing paintball, rock climbing, and going to the movies are popular in Nairobi. However, since many Kenyans are poor, they often make their own fun at home. Bao is a popular, low-cost board game that involves moving seeds or stones around a board.

**Boa is played all over the world. In other places, it's known as mancala, oware, sungka, and many other names.**

## OLYMPIC ATHLETES

Kenya is home to some of the world's top athletes. Kenya has won 35 gold medals, 42 silver medals, and 36 bronze medals at the Olympic Games, as of 2023.

# FOOD

Breakfast isn't as popular in Kenya as it is in the United States. Many Kenyans start their day with a cup of milky, sweetened tea and a piece of bread or fruit. Lunch and dinner are bigger meals, and Kenyans often eat with family and friends.

**FACT!**

Kenyans cook corn on the cob inside its husk, or outer leaves, over a fire and sell it as a popular street food.

This roadside stand sells fruits that grow in Kenya.

Kenyans eat *ugali* at many meals. This is a thick **porridge** made from corn flour and water. Ugali is cheap, but also healthy. Kenyans serve it with vegetables or meat. Goat is the most commonly eaten meat.

Near the coast, Kenyans eat more fish. Different ethnic groups have their own preferred foods too. For example, the Kikuyu tend to eat more corn, beans, and a kind of seed called lentils.

## FANCY RICE

Kenyans eat rice plain except on special days, such as holidays or weddings. Then, they cook it with spices, nuts, and dried fruits. This dish is called pilau rice.

This plate holds a common Kenyan meal of fish, kale stew, and ugali.

# GLOSSARY

**ancestor:** A family member who lived long ago.

**cabinet:** A group of advisers that helps the leader of a government.

**climate:** The weather over a long period of time.

**constitution:** A document that sets down the rules of a country.

**continent:** One of the main landmasses on Earth.

**economy:** The way goods and services are made and sold.

**engrave:** To cut a word or design into a hard surface with a sharp object.

**equator:** An imaginary horizontal line running around the center of Earth.

**ethnic group:** A group of people who share a common background and way of life.

**fossil:** A trace or print or the remains of a plant or animal of a past age preserved in earth or rock.

**nomadic:** Having no permanent home.

**porridge:** A soft food made by boiling a powder, such as flour or corn, in milk or water until it thickens.

**reserve:** A piece of public land set aside as a place to keep certain plants and animals safe.

**savanna:** A grassland with very few trees.

# FIND OUT MORE

## Books

Davies, Monika. *Kenya*. Minneapolis, MN: Bellwether Media, 2023.

Doeden, Matt. *Travel to Kenya*. Minneapolis, MN: Lerner Publications, 2022.

Duling, Kaitlyn. *Your Passport to Kenya*. North Mankato, MN: Capstone Press, 2021.

## Websites

**Kids World Travel Guide: Kenya**
*www.kids-world-travel-guide.com/facts-about-kenya.html*
Learn some Kiswahili words, and take a look at some cool pictures of Kenya!

***National Geographic Kids*: Kenya**
*kids.nationalgeographic.com/geography/countries/article/kenya*
Learn more about Kenya's geography, government, and history.

## Video

**YouTube: How Flip-Flop Art Helps Clean Kenya's Beaches**
*www.youtube.com/watch?v=GK-BHZs7GxE&t=329s*
Watch how Ocean Sole turns trash into art.

# INDEX